ELLA

Diaries

TOP SECRET!

With special thanks to Cristina, Mewanmi,
Gwyneth, Isabel, Ananya and Sucheta from
Boroondara Park Primary School—M.C.

Meredith Costain

For my pirate crew—
Zoe, Jade and Ray—D.M.

Danielle McDonald

First American Edition 2018
Kane Miller, A Division of EDC Publishing

Text copyright © Meredith Costain, 2016
Illustrations copyright © Danielle McDonald, 2016

First published by Scholastic Australia, a division of Scholastic Australia Pty Limited in
2016. This edition published under license from Scholastic Australia Pty Limited.

For information contact:
Kane Miller, A Division of EDC Publishing
PO Box 470663
Tulsa, OK 74147-0663
www.kanemiller.com
www.edcpub.com
www.usbornebooksandmore.com

Library of Congress Control Number: 2018932770

Printed and bound in the United States of America

1 2 3 4 5 6 7 8 9 10

ISBN: 978-1-61067-836-0

ELLA
Diaries

FRIENDS NOT FOREVER

Kane Miller
A DIVISION OF EDC PUBLISHING

Monday night, in bed, just before lights-out

Dear Diary,

TWO very thrilling and mysterious things happened at school today.

Thrilling AND Mysterious THING

NUMBER ONE

There is a new girl in our class. Her name is Amethyst Merryweather.

Amethyst Merryweather

These are the things I know
about her:

 She is VERY quiet.

 She doesn't like answering questions
about herself.

That's it. (Hopefully I will have more to
report about this tomorrow. ☺)

Thrilling AND Mysterious THING

NUMBER TWO

Our lovely and excellent teacher Ms. Weiss announced that something **very exciting** is going to be happening at school soon. Something we will LOVE.

So then we all tried to guess what it is. Here are our Top Seven guesses:

Guesser	Guess	Chance of being correct (with reasons)
ME	A famous celebrity (like my favorite pop singer, Cassi Valentine!) is coming to our school.	99.9% Please, please, please, please, pretty please be true!
ZOE	We are getting a horse to be our class pet.	50% We had baby chicks last year, and a horse is just another type of farm animal. Although where would it sit?

Guesser	Guess	Chance of being correct (with reasons)
GEORGIA	We are going to stop being a real school and become a pirate school instead, and everyone is going to learn cool stuff like how to draw treasure maps and say "Arrrr." ARRRRRR!	**5%** Mr. Martini would NEVER let this happen. Though I do like the idea of drawing treasure maps. Treasure MAP

Raf	Everyone in our class is going to Mars with our own personal jet packs.	**O%** Anyone with even a tiny brain knows that there are no stores or oxygen on Mars and we would ALL DIE!!!
Peter	All the teachers at our school (including the principal, Mr. Martini) have turned into zombies and have to go to a special zombie treatment facility to be un-zombified.	**O%** If our teachers were really zombies, according to the Rules of Zombiedom, we'd all be zombies by now too! ZOMBIE

Guesser	Guess	Chance of being correct (with reasons)
ALI	Our school is going to close down for the next two weeks!	**0.1%** This is just silly. Unless all the bathrooms blew up. (But then again, we'd already know if that happened!)
Zac	Our school is going to close down for the next two years!!! Toilets	0.0000000001% This is even sillier. It would never take that long to fix the bathrooms, even if they were smashed into teeny tiny pieces.

Ms. Weiss said all our guesses were wrong. But then she said one of them was actually VERY CLOSE to the REAL thrilling and mysterious thing!

Ms. Weiss

And she was just about to tell us what it was when the bell started ringing!

RINGG!

RINGG!

And sirens started blaring!

WOOP!
WOOP!
WOOP!

And all the little kids from the baby classes ran out into the playground screaming their heads off, while Mrs. Gupta and Mr. Bing tried to herd them into lines.

And then Mrs. Cardamone ran along the corridor with a megaphone saying, "Fire Drill! Fire Drill! Please make your way to the covered area and wait with your class."

And we all had to hold hands
with a partner, like BABIES,
and walk out quietly to the
covered area and line up in rows.

HOLD
HANDS

ME!

LIKE BaBIES

~~Unforch~~ Unfortunately, some
of the boys from my class
(especially Peter and Raf) thought this would
be a really good time to start behaving like
zombies. They made their eyes roll around
in their eye sockets and said things like
"Brains, brains!" and clutched each other's
throats like zombies do.

RAF →   Peter   BRAINS!
BRAINS!

Ms. Weiss was NOT amused. So as soon as the fire drill finished and we all came back to class, she made us do a spelling pop quiz with extra-hard words on it, like RESPONSIBLE and RELIABLE and SENSIBLE and ~~MACHEWER~~ MATURE, until the *real* bell went for the end of school.

Ms. Weiss

So I STILL don't know what the thrilling and mysterious thing is. Or which of the seven ideas was the very close one.

I hope it was mine!!!

Or Zoe's!!

Or maybe it is both of them mixed up
together, and Cassi Valentine is going to
come to our school
on a horse and give
us all horseback
riding lessons!

Cassi
Valentine

I can't wait to FIND OUT

Good night, Diary.
Sweet dreams.
Ella xx

Tuesday, after school

Dear Diary,

Ms. Weiss FINALLY told us the thrilling and mysterious news this morning.

We're going to be doing a SCHOOL PLAY! And she and Mr. Zugaro (my second-most favorite teacher, because he likes my poetry) are going to be organizing it. YAY!!!

Ms. Weiss

Mr. Zugaro

I love school plays. I was just about to put up my hand and tell Ms. Weiss how happy I was about the play, when Precious Princess Peach Parker, who is the most annoying person in the history of annoyingness and also a SUPER ICKY teacher's pet, put up her hand and said, "Oooooooooooo. We're so LUCKY! I LOVE being in school plays. What's it going to be about, Ms. Weiss?"

· PRECIOUS · PEACH · PARKER ·

And then Ms. Weiss gave Princess Peach one of her special smiles, which is SOOO unfair, because it should have been ME who got the special smile. ☹

SOOO UNFAIR

And then she turned back to the class and said, "Remember how I said one of the guesses you made yesterday was VERY CLOSE?"

And then Peter and Raf called out, "Zombies! Yesss!"

They were just jumping up to do their zombie dance again when they saw the look on Ms. Weiss's face and said, "Oops. Sorry, Ms. Weiss." Then they sat down again before she gave us another spelling test.

MS. WEISS

Then Ms. Weiss said
that, actually, the play
wasn't going to be
about zombies. Or us
going to Mars with our
own personal jet packs.
Or the school closing
down. Or a class-pet
horse.

It was going to be about . . .

Drumroll . . .

Pirates

We're going to do a play set on a pirate ship, with lots of **singing** and **dancing**, called Pirates of the Caribooboo.

There's going to be a **piratical pirate** called Captain Swashbuckler, who is the Scourge✱ of the Seven Seas.

✱ A scourge is something that causes great trouble or suffering. Like a pesky mosquito with **gigantic** bitey parts. Or Olivia, my little sister. You say it like this—skerrj.

pesky
(OLIVIA)
mosquito

There's also a fabulously fabulous character in the play called Mabel Diggs that I would be PERFECT for!

She sings. ✓

And dances. ✓

And does pirate stuff like sword fighting. ✓

And Ms. Weiss said the girl who plays Mabel gets to wear lots of different super-stylish costumes. ✓✓✓

I have to be Mabel. I just HAVE to!
And besides all the main pirate roles, there are going to be ship's rats, and a ship's cat called Tiddles to chase them, and a talking parrot named Polly.

RATS

Tiddles

Here is a list of the main characters:

Pirates *of* THE CARIBOOBOO
CHARACTER LIST:

CAPTAIN
Swashbuckler
THE SCOURGE OF THE SEVEN SEAS

Mabel Diggs *
A MYSTERIOUS MEMBER OF THE CREW

← Tommy KNUCKLE
the FIRST MATE that has a heart of gold

Dennis DOOLITTLE
a lazy pirate --->

←--DENISE DOOLITTLER
another lazy pirate

POLLY
↳ THE PARROT

TIDDLES
THE SHIP'S CAT

It's going to be **excellently excellent**. I can't wait!

I have to stop writing now, Diary, because Zoe is coming over so we can have an

EMERGENCY meeting

about the play, and I haven't made the KEEP OUT sign for my bedroom door yet.

If I don't make the sign, Olivia will think she can come in again and start rearranging things on my desk. And my bookshelves. And repeat everything we say (including our most secret secrets) to her friend Matilda, who will then blab our secrets to all her friends, JUST LIKE SHE DID LAST TIME!

Bye.
Love, Ella

Tuesday, after school, fifteen minutes later

Still waiting for Zoe to turn up.

Here is a picture of the sign I made. I used three different gel pens. It's the best one ever! ☺☺☺

Tuesday night, after dinner

Dearest Diary,

Zoe finally turned up! Phew. When we were absolutely totally completely utterly **100%** sure that Olivia wasn't snooping on us by sitting on the other side of the door with a drinking glass, we started our meeting.

INSIDE MY BEDROOM

This is what we said:

Me: Pirates of the Caribooboo is going to be EXcellent.

   Zoe: I know.
   Me: You and I are PERFECT for this play. We're both going to get main roles for sure.

Zoe: I know. It's so exciting!

Me (casually): Which part are you going for?

Me (silently, inside my brain):

Please don't say Mabel.

Please don't say Mabel.

Please don't say Mabel.

Zoe: Maybe one of the animals?

Like Tiddles the Cat? I don't want one of

the big speaking parts. What if I forget
my lines on stage? It would be sooo
embarrassing!

Me (inside my brain again): *Phew.*

Zoe: What about you?

Me: Mabel. In fact, I am
desperately desperate to be
Mabel. I hope we get lots of
scenes together.

Zoe: Same.

Inside MY BRAIN

PHEW.

We were in the middle of planning our
thank-you speeches (for when people come
up onto the stage at the end of the play to
give us flowers) when we heard a muffled
noise, which sounded ~~suspish~~ suspiciously like

Olivia dropping a glass on the carpet outside my door, and then someone saying "Oops."

This is what happened next:

Me: I can hear you out there, O-liv-ia.
Muffled sound: Nnmnoyoomnncannt.
Me: Yes, I can. You're SNOOPING on us.
Muffled sound: Nnmnolmmnmnot.
Me: YES YOU ARE! Now STOP BEING A PAIN AND GO AWAY!
Olivia: I'm SOOO telling Mom on you!

Sisters! They are SOOOO infuriating!

After that Zoe and I didn't feel like planning thank-you speeches anymore. So we had fun doing pirate things like practicing our "Arrrrs" and dancing the sailor's hornpipe* instead.

HORNPIPE

* The hornpipe is a type of jumpy dance that sailors do, with folded arms and lots of kicky leg moves.

And then we dressed Bob up like a pirate.
Here is a picture of what he looked like.
Doesn't he look sweet?

Dad's
Shoes →

Pirate
BOB

I am SO LUCKY to have a BFF like Zoe. I
wish she was my sister. Then she could live
here all the time and I'd never be annoyed
or infuriated or snooped on ever again.

Good night, Diary.
Talk tomorrow.
E xx

Wednesday night, just before lights-out

Hey, Diary,

Guess what? Today we found out some more interesting facts about the Mysterious Amethyst Merryweather.

INTERESTING FACTS ABOUT AMETHYST

Amethyst's **NOSE**

BOOK

1 She LOVES reading and always has her nose in a book. Especially at lunchtime, when everyone else is running madly around the playground like mad things.

2 She doesn't like sandwiches. (I discovered this when I **kindly** offered her one of my ~~gormay~~ gourmet chicken liver with chopped egg and beets sandwiches at lunchtime today—so she wouldn't feel so **lonely** and **new**—and she went all pale and looked like she was going to throw up.)

Gourmet SANDWICH

— chicken **Liver**

---- CHOPPED **EGG**

--- **BEEts**

3 She always wears something that is purple, like a hair ribbon or shoelaces. Cordelia (who also loves reading and knows lots of interesting stuff) says this is

PURPLE ribbon

because amethysts are ~~fools~~ jewels that are purple.

AMETHYST = PURPLE jewel

4 She must get into trouble A LOT.✳ I saw her sitting outside Mr. Martini's office THREE WHOLE TIMES this week. And she didn't look happy when I asked her why she was sitting there. Especially the THIRD time I asked her.

✳ It must be for doing something like running in the school corridor or writing rude words on the wall in the girls' bathroom because she NEVER EVER gets into trouble in class. Ever.

PRINCIPAL

← MR. MARTiNi's OFFICE

And guess what else?
The auditions for the
play start on Monday!
We're going to get our scripts tomorrow
and we have to choose a part and practice
saying some of our lines. Then at the
audition we will read them out in front of
the part choosers.

I am going to practice my lines ALL
WEEKEND!

Good night, Diary.
Love, Ella xx

★AUDITIONS★
MONDAY

Script

Thursday morning, very, very early

Dear Diary,

I just had the **best dream!**

We were doing the play and I was Mabel and I had my own private, personal dressing room with a star on the door, like this:

And people kept walking past and leaving
me gigantic bunches of flowers

and there were newspaper and TV reporters
wanting to interview me

and thousands of people were screaming
out my name

and lining up to get my autograph.

It was aMAZing.

Love, (Celebrity) Ella

Friday morning, early

Guess what? I had the dream about being Mabel AGAIN!

Maybe this means it's all going to come true. I CAN'T WAIT!!

Friday night, late

Dear Diary,

I am so ANGRY I want to SCREAM!

Really, really LOUDLY!!

Like this!

This is what happened at school today.

Zoe and I were quietly working on our Famous Pirates through History projects,✳ and I was telling her all about my aMAZing dreams. And I was up to the part about how everyone wanted my autograph when I heard this sniggery, snorty sound right beside me.

✳ Ms. Weiss thought it would be fun to do pirate projects in class because of our school play. Mine's about this lady river pirate from the olden days called Sadie the Goat.

SADIE THE GOAT

(River PiRATE)

And guess who it was?

Perfect Princess Peach Parker. She was
standing next to our table
with a big sneery smirk
all over her face.

BiG
Sneery
SMiRK

So I said, "Can I help you?"

And she said, "I don't know. Can you?"

Then she handed me this scratchy, old glitter
pen THAT WASN'T EVEN MINE and said
in this really fake voice, "I found this on the
floor, and while I've been waiting for you
to stop talking so I could give it to you, I
accidentally overheard you telling Zoe how
you're going to be Mabel in the play."

And then before I could say anything, she looked down her nose at me and said, "Ha! Like that's ever going to happen," and went back to her friends.

Peach is such a SNOOP! And a MEANIE! I sat there staring straight ahead, getting more and more furious, thinking of all the things I wanted to say to her.

Zoe put her arm around me and said, "Don't listen to her, Ella. You can be **anything** you want to be and she can't stop you."

And then she showed me this really fancy way to do a heading for my Sadie the Goat project, with little curly goat horns coming out of the G.

GOAT HORNS

And then I helped her write a funny poem
about her pirate, Blackbeard.

Blackbeard's beard
Was really weird
And darker than the night
He looked into a mirror once
And gave himself a fright!

Blackbeard's
BEARD!

And then we told each other funny pirate jokes, like:

Q. What is a pirate's favorite subject at pirate school?
A. ARRRRT!

and

Q. What are pirates afraid of?
A. THE DAAAAAARK!

and

Q. Why are pirates called pirates?
A. They just ARRRRRR!

And then we kept saying
ARRRRRRRRR! over and over
and we laughed and laughed till
we got tummy aches and our
faces
hurt, and Ms. Weiss had to tell
us to stop being silly and get
on with our work.

Ha HA
ha

Laughing and being silly with Zoe made me
feel A LOT better.

But I still want to SCREAM!!!!

Saturday night, just before lights-out

Dear Diary-doo,

Guess what?!

Nanna Kate took Zoe and me to the movies at the shopping center today as a special treat for helping her with the weeding. (Nanna Kate HATES weeding. Especially when she finds squished snails on the stalks with bits of their guts hanging out. Eww.)

Eww!

Squished SNAIL

out. Eww.)
Unfortunately, Olivia and Max came along too, even though they didn't do any weeding. It's SO UNFAIR!

MAX

Zoe and I REALLY wanted to see the new pirate movie called The Pirate Princess, but Max made us late because he kept stopping all the time to look at bugs, and by the time we got there it was SOLD OUT!

The PIRATE

SOLD OUT

Princess

NOOOO·····

So we had to see this BABY movie made for BABIES instead.

When the movie finished Zoe and I went to the food court, while Nanna Kate took Olivia and Max to the bathroom so they'd stop whining about wanting to go all the time. (Everyone kept looking at us while they were doing the whining. It was SO EMBARRASSING!)

And guess what?

You never will so I'll just tell you.

We accidentally bumped into
Peach at the ice cream shop.
NOOOOOOOOOOOOOOOOOO!

She was with her best
buddies, Jade and Prinny.

They were all wearing
matchy-matchy outfits.
Even their ice cream
was matchy.

matchy - matchy

BLEUCHhh.

"Oh, look," said Peach (fake) sweetly to her friends. "It's Mold-y May-belle."

And then they all laughed like hyenas who had caught a laughing disease.

Zoe glared at them glaringly. Then she said, "What's your problem? Ella can be Mabel if she wants to."

Peach gave me one of her creepy crocodile smiles. Then she came up really close to me, so close I could practically see up her nose. Eww.

CREEPY CROCODILE SMILE

This is what we all said next:

Peach: I hope you know all your lines, Mold-y May-belle.
Me: What do you mean?
Zoe: Yeah, what do you mean?

Peach: You have to know all your lines **by heart** for the audition.
Prinny: Yeah.
Jade: Yeah.
Zoe: No we don't. We can just read them off the script. Ms. Weiss said.

Peach: That's what EVERYONE ELSE who wants to be Mabel will be doing.
Me: So?

Peach (moving in even closer): But if you REALLY want the part, you have to do something extra to show you're more special than them.

Me (suspiciously): Are you learning your lines?

Peach (innocently): Of course! Prinny and Jade have been helping me, haven't you, Prinny and Jade?

Prinny and Jade (together): Yeah.

Zoe (even more suspiciously): So which part are you going for?

Peach: Ummm . . . Denise Doodah. I mean Doodad. I mean Doolittler. Yeah, her. Anyway, we have to go now. Tootles!

Prinny and Jade (together): Yeah, tootles!

And then they walked
off with smirky
smirks all over their
smirky faces.

I was just about to call another Emergency
Meeting with Zoe to discuss what we should
do about knowing our lines when Nanna
Kate came back with Max and Olivia.

So we're going to have it tomorrow instead.

Love,
Ella x

Sunday, after dinner

Dear Diary,

Zoe and I spent the WHOLE DAY getting ready for our auditions tomorrow. It was the BEST Emergency Meeting in the history of Emergency Meetings!

Here's what we did:

1. Phoned Olivia's best friend Matilda and convinced her, with candy and glitter pens, to invite Olivia over to her house, so she couldn't snoop on us again.

Matilda

2 Practiced our sword fighting.

3 Talked like pirates in pirate voices.

4 Said our lines from the play over and over **AND OVER** again until we knew them by heart. Mine were **MUCH** harder to remember than Zoe's.

I'm Mabel **Diggs** from **Violet** Town, **A** sassy **Lass,** **that's** ME. **A** **Pirate's** Life is **ALL** I want, So I Ran **away** to **Sea.**

ME as Mabel

Goodnight, Diary.

Ella

xoxox

Sunday night, very late

Dearest Diary,

I am WAY too excited about the auditions to sleep. So I wrote this shape poem about being a star instead.

A
star
twinkles
and shines
in the sky and
lights up the world.
Star light star bright here's the wish I wish tonight:
I wish I could be Mabel in the school play and
sing and act and dance and have a star
on my dressing room door and
people would clap and cheer
and bring me flowers.
A star glows and gleams
and brings joy to everyone.
I want to be a shining star!
A glistening   glimmering
sparkly   glittery
shiny   star.

Wish me good luck for tomorrow, Diary!

Love,
Ella xoxox

Monday, straight after school

Dear Diary,

I am SHOCKED!

So shocked I can't write anything about what happened right now.

Maybe later, after I've had a nice calming walk with Bob in the park.

In disguise. In case I bump into someone I don't want to see or talk to.

E

SHOCK Horror

Monday, about half an hour later

Nope. Still too shocked to write.

Monday, about ten minutes after that

Maybe I'll be able to write something after dinner—if I am still alive then. I may have died of an extreme case of Despairing Despair Disease. The one that makes all your teeth and toenails and heart fall out. At least then I will have an ~~exyou~~ excuse not to go to school tomorrow.
Because I am never EVER going back to school.

Ever.

☹☹☹☹

Despairing DESPAIR ~~Des~~ Disease

Monday night, in bed

Dearest Diary,

Max came in just now with a comforting hot water bottle, plus half* an old stale Easter egg he found at the back of his toy cupboard, and gave them to me because he thought I looked sad.

* Max already ate the other half.

Maybe I can write a little bit about what happened today.

WARNING: This next bit is exTREMEly sad and tragic. You may need tissues.

Zoe and I arrived at school **super early** so we could write our names on the auditions list before it filled up with other people wanting the same parts as us.

Pirates of The CARibooboo
AUDITIONS

Where: Ethel Morman Memorial Gym

When: 1:15 pm SHARP!

Please write your name here:

Daniel Ratcliffy

Peach Parker

Prinny Aquino

Harry Spotter

Jade Snyder

Johnno Depp

- - - - - - - - -

- - - - - - - - -

We added our names then ran off to our special place under the cypress trees to do some more practicing.

When school finally started, Ms. Weiss had to tell us both THREE TIMES to "settle down, please." But we were too fizzy with EXCITEMENT. We couldn't wait for it to be lunchtime so we could show the directors how FABULOUSLY FABULOUS we were!

At lunchtime, we went to the gym at 1:15 p.m. sharp, just like the notice said. But . . .

Da-da-da . . .

Dummmmmm.

There was nobody there.

Bleuchhh!

Peach

Precious Princess Peach Parker had tricked us.

AGAIN! WAAAAHHH!

The notice was FAKE! Fake! FAKe!

Even the names on it were FAKE!

Harry Spotter doesn't even go to our school. How emBARRassing! Anyone with even a tiny brain knows that!

So then we ran **madly** around the school like **mad things**, trying to find out where the REAL audition place was before lunchtime finished and we missed out on being Mabel and Tiddles forever. ☹

MAD THings

We were just about to
give up and spend the rest
of our lives in despairing
despair when we saw Cordelia coming out
of a room with a sign on it that said:

PLAY AUDITIONS
THIS WAY ★
→

And guess what?

The auditions were still going!

YESSSs!!

You're probably thinking that everything that happened after that was fabulously fabulous and there was a happy ending, just like in a fairy tale.

Shiny EYES

Happy FACES

A HAPPY fairy tale

WRONG! WRONG! WRONG!

There was no happy ending.

In fact it was the saddest ending in the history of endings. ☹☹☹☹

I have to stop for a bit now, so I can get some more tissues. And maybe some chocolate chip cookies. And some ice cream—with chocolate sprinkles. I'll be right back . . .

Monday night, about two minutes later

ONE chocolate CHIP cookie

Sadly, Mom said I was only allowed to have one cookie and no ice cream (with or without sprinkles), because all that rich food so close to bedtime would be bad for me and might give me nightmares.
That is SO unfair!
I bet Princess Peach is allowed to have ice cream (with sprinkles!) any time she wants.✳ ☹

Bleuchhh!

✳ Actually, I hope she does have ice cream and does have nightmares. Scary ones with big, hairy, googly-eyed monsters in them. (I know that makes me sound mean, but I am too ~~DISTRORT~~ DISTRAUGHT to care anymore.)

So back to the story . . . Zoe and I sat down on the chairs, waiting for it to be our turn, watching all the other kids reading out bits of the play.

Most of them were **hopelessly hopeless**, ~~exp~~ especially Don Tay.✱ Don Tay is this boy who was in our class at ballet school. In fact, he was the *only* boy in our class at ballet school. He was also the only boy at the auditions, which means he is guaranteed 100% sure to get a part. It's so not fair. ☹

✱ His real name is actually Dante, but we didn't know that until we saw it on a list one day. Oops!

Don **Tay**

But guess what? There was one girl who was exCEPtionally excellent at acting. She was so good everyone stopped whispering to each other and thinking When's it going to be MY turn? and stared at her with shiny eyes and said, "Zow-ee, she is aMAZing."

Guess who it was? You never will in a million trillion years, so I'll just tell you.

It was Amethyst Merryweather!
She is what my Nanna Kate
calls a dark horse.** Which
makes her EVEN MORE
mysterious. I wonder how she
got so good at acting?

★AMETHYST★
MERRYWEATHER

** A dark horse isn't actually a horse
at all. It is a person who everyone thinks
is hopelessly hopeless at something, like
playing the bagpipes or winning spitting
competitions, but they are in fact
fabulously fabulous at it
and everyone says, "Ooo!
What a big surprise.
I am SHOCKED."

DARK horse

All that sitting
and waiting made
me more and more
nervous. I was so
nervous there were
butterflies doing
the cancan in my
tummy.

Butterflies DOING THE CANCAN

IN MY TUMMY

And then all of a sudden Ms. Weiss called
out Zoe's name and asked her which part
she wanted to be. And Zoe got mixed up
and said "Meow?" instead of "Tiddles, the
ship's cat."

And everybody laughed.

Then Zoe did a few more meows and pretended to do that thing cats do when they lick their paws then rub them behind their ears, and then she pranced around like a real cat and everyone laughed again. Especially Ms. Weiss and Mr. Zugaro, who had gigantic smiles on their faces the whole time she was acting and kept giving each other "meaningful looks," like this:

MS. WEISS

MR. ZUGARO

Amethyst gave Zoe a **gigantic smile** as well, like it was the **best thing** she'd ever seen.

And then Zoe sat down again with a big "PHEWW" and it was my turn.

Mr. Zugaro gave me a script to read from but I said, "No, thank you very much, I don't need one. I know my part by heart."

And then something horrifically horrible happened. So horrifically horrible I wanted the floor to open up so I could disappear down into the deep, dark ground so no one could ever see me again. Not even if they had a light on their head, like miners do.

So horrifically horrible I can hardly write it down, because then it will be true.

I forgot my lines. ☹

Everyone was staring at me, waiting for me to start. But I couldn't remember Mabel's speech, even though I'd practiced it with Zoe about 900 times. So I made something up instead.

Mabel's speech (the real one)

I'm Mabel Diggs from Violet Town,
A sassy lass, that's me.
A pirate's life is all I want,
So I ran away to sea.

What I ~~Ack~~ Actually Said

Hello, my name is Mabel Piggs and I . . . (mumble mumble) . . . I like . . . umm . . . pirate stuff. And running.

And then everybody laughed. Only it wasn't nice, friendly laughing, like they did when Zoe was being a cat. It was mean, horrid, horrible, NASTY laughing.

And guess who was laughing the nastiest?

HINT: Her name rhymes with speech.

Princess Peach is a LIAR, LIAR, PANTS ON FIRE.

She didn't know her part by heart either. She just read her lines from the script, like all the other people auditioning.

It was all just a **big, mean, nasty-pasty TRICK** to make me look bad.

And guess which part she tried out for?

HINT: It rhymes with table.

NOoooooooO !

Why, Diary? WHY?????

Tuesday, after school

Dear Diary,

I am **STILL** shocked!

Ms. Weiss and Mr. Zugaro put up a "callback" list of people they wanted to see again before they decided on the main parts.

Zoe's name was on the list.

And Don Tay's.
And Cordelia's.
And Mysterious Amethyst's.

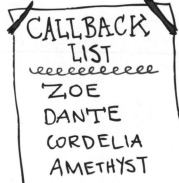

Mine wasn't.

I was just about to creep away to die
a **slow** and **lingering tragic desperate
death** under the cypress trees when Zoe
discovered another list, right next to the
first one.

And the heading at the
top said DANCERS.

The Good News
My name was right at
the **top** of the list!

The Bad News

Princess Peach's name was right underneath mine. And so were Prinny's and Jade's. And then the names of all the gym girls who do gymnastics at lunchtime, with their hair pulled back into tight little buns—in case it gets caught in the gym equipment and then their heads EXPLODE.

HAIR!

GYM equip- ment

GYMNAST

The Not So Bad News That Made Me Feel a Bit Better

And then underneath their names were the names of my other friends, like Georgia and Chloe and Daisy and Poppy. So we are all going to be dancers in the play together. YAY!

But it's SO NOT FAIR, Diary. I really, really, REALLY wanted to be Mabel.

And now someone else is going to be her instead.

AND IT'S ALL PEACH PARKER'S FAULT!

Wednesday night, in bed, just before lights-out

Dear Diary,

Today was the ~~worserest~~ worst day of my life.

EVER!!

Here's what happened.

I went with Zoe to the callbacks, even though I was desperately sad that my two favorite teachers in the WHOLE WORLD hadn't chosen me—because that is the kind of thing BFFs do. And because I was happy for Zoe that she'd been chosen, even though I was SEETHING with ENVY. (And also because Ms. Weiss said there were going to be snacks.)

ENVY

Seething (ME)

Mr. Zugaro called up all the callback people one by one to read the different parts. Then he and Ms. Weiss asked us to wait quietly (ha!) while they had a BIG DISCUSSION.

While we were waiting (un)quietly, Amethyst came over. Amethyst! The same Amethyst who never speaks. Ever.

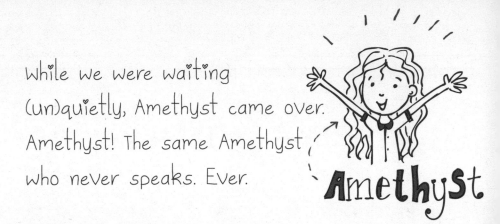

Amethyst

This is what we✳ said:

✳ ~~Actsh~~ Actually, this is what Amethyst and Zoe said. I didn't get a chance to say ANYthing.

Amethyst: Hey, Zoe. You were really good.
Zoe (going all red): Umm, no I wasn't.
Everyone laughed.
Amethyst: Because you were REALLY FUNNY. You were aMAZing.

Zoe (going all redder): ☺

Amethyst: You should have gone for one of the main parts, like Denise or Mabel.

Zoe (shocked): No way! I'd mess up all my lines.

Amethyst: No you wouldn't. You'd be great! I think—

Sadly, we never did get to find out what Amethyst thinks, because Ms. Weiss and Mr. Zugaro finished their big discussion, and said they were ready to give out the main parts. All the actors stopped being (un)quiet and stood there, staring up at them with **shiny eyes**, waiting to find out if they got one.

EVERYone thought Don Tay would get Captain Swashbuckler, the biggest of all the main parts.

But guess what? He didn't. Amethyst did! Don Tay will be Tommy Knuckle instead.

And guess which part Zoe got?

(If you guessed Tiddles the Cat you are WRONG!

WRONG!

WRONG!)

TiddLes

POLLY

CORDELIA

GRACE

★MABEL★

She was shocked! But also really happy.

Then all the people with main parts had to line up so Ms. Weiss could take their photo.

Tommy

CAPTAIN
Swashbuckler

MABEL

Dennis

Denise

DON TAY

★AMETHYST★
MERRYWEATHER

ZOE

Maddy

Zeynep

And then they stayed there chatting and having fun when the bell rang and everyone else (including me ☹) had to go back to class.

Good night, Diary.
E

Thursday, after school

Dear Diary,

Today we started our
dance rehearsals with
Ms. Crosby. I was

Ms. CROSBY

hoping Zoe might come to watch like I did
for her, but she said she would be too busy
with her OWN rehearsal. With the ACTors.

And then she said,

I'll come next time.
I Promise.

So that's
OK then.

OUR rehearsal was EXcellent!

There are two groups of dancers.

Group A

Group A (the best dancers) are
the crew of the pirate ship.
They are going to do lots of
complicated dances with ropes
and mops and even **sword
fighting!** And one dancer gets
to do a special dance called a
pas de deux* with one of the
actors!

* A *pas de deux* is a dance for two people. You say it like this—pah de der. I learned how to dance them at ballet school. You do leaps and twirls and arabesques where you stick your back leg up really high in the air.

Group B

Group B (the not-so-good dancers) are the ship's rats. They are going to do a funny dance where they get chased around the deck by Tiddles.

Tiddles

RATS

We all held our breath and crossed our fingers and toes while we waited for Ms. Crosby to tell us which group we were in.

The Good News

I'm in **GROUP A**

YAY!

The Bad News

So are Princess Peach and Prinny and Jade and all the stuck-up gym-bun girls. ☹

Wahh...!

The Worse News

All my second-best friends like Georgia and
Poppy and Daisy and Chloe are in Group B.
Which means I won't have anyone to have
fun with when we're rehearsing. ☹☹☹

Then Ms. Crosby said there is going to be
an **extra-special** dancing audition to see
who gets to dance the pas de deux.

I **really, really** want to win!

I have to go now so I can practice my leaps
and twirls and arabesques for tomorrow.

Wish me luck, Diary!
Love,
Ella xx

Thursday, about fifteen minutes later

Dear Diary,

Well, I just called Zoe to see if she wanted to come over to my house to help me practice for the pas de deux auditions. And **guess what?** She said she couldn't because she was already doing something. with ANOTHER FRIEND.

So I had to practice my pas de deux with a chair. ☹☹☹ .

CHAIR

ME

Friday night, in bed

Dear, darlingest Diary,

We had the pas de deux auditions today and we all had to do a really tricky dance to show off our ~~teckneek~~ technique. I wore my best tutu and did a dance I learned at ballet school. It looked like this:

This time the butterflies in my stomach were doing the cha-cha-cha. I really, REALLY wanted Zoe to be there to watch me dance for good luck but she just smiled a little smile and said, "Sorry, Ella, not today. I have a big scene to rehearse with someone else."

What???!

But guess what?

ELLA!

Ms. Crosby chose ME
to do the pas de deux,
even without Zoe's
good luck!

Not Peach, or Prinny or Jade.

★ME!★

And I get to change out of the boring
striped T-shirt and baggy pants and
bandana that all the ship's crew wear and
into a stylish floaty
costume for my
special dance.

striped T-Shirt

BANDANA

Baggy Pants

It is going to be AWESOME!

Except for one tiny problem.

The person I am dancing the
pas de deux with is . . .

Don Tay

Last time Don Tay
danced a pas de deux it
was with Esther Grech in
our ballet performance
pick
UP
and TWIRL
and he got all tangled up in her floaty
dress when he picked her up and twirled her
around over his head. And then he dropped
her and Esther broke her
big toe in two places and
had to go to the hospital
in an ~~amber~~ ambulance.

AMBULANCE

WAAAAHhh!

Good night,
Ella

Saturday night, in bed, very late

Dear Diary,

I am in desperate despair.
☹

I called Zoe this morning to see if she wanted to come over so we could work on ideas for my floaty costume for my big dance scene. Zoe always has **excellently excellent** ideas for things like that.

Her mom said she'd gone to the movies WITH **A FRIEND** and she was going to be out **ALL DAY**, but maybe we could catch up tomorrow. And she would get Zoe to call me back.

And I said (casually), "Oh that's nice. Did she say what movie?"

And her mom said, "Yes, she did. It was a **lovely movie** all about pirates called *The Pirate Princess.*"

The movie I wanted to see last Saturday. With Zoe. **My BFF.**

☹☹☹☹☹☹☹

Saturday night, a bit later

Which friend??????

Sunday, after lunch

I waited ALL morning for
Zoe to call me back.

She didn't.

Zoe and I always call each
other at least 900 times
on the weekend. ESPECially
on Sunday mornings. ☹

I must be the only person in the WHOLE WORLD who doesn't have someone to talk to. I couldn't even talk to Olivia because she was HAVING FUN at her friend Matilda's house. ALL DAY.

BORED

I am stuck in my room dying of boredom, Diary! In fact I am SO BORED I am extremely surprised my head hasn't exploded.

1 2 3 4 5 6 7 8 9 10

Not Very BORED

Kind OF BORED

EXTREMELY BORED
to THE POWER of
1,000,000

So I worked on ideas for my costume with Max.

Yours in desperation,
Ella

PS He wasn't very helpful.

Max's favorite CAP

Max's FAVORITE Toys hanging from SLEEVES

DAd's BeLt

Mom's Saggy Baggy "JUST FOR AROUND THE HOUSE" HiPPY PANTS

Sunday evening, just before dinner

Dear Diary,

Everything is hopelessly hopeless. I am so devastatingly distraught I think I might die a slow and tragic death extremely soon. (Though probably not till after dinner because we are having spaghetti, my favorite.)

Here is a list of things I am bequeathing✳ to my family and (ex)BFFs after I die:

Yum!

Name	What I am bequeathing them
Dad	Gerald, my (latest) pet praying mantis
Mom	My butterfly hairclips
Olivia	My gel and glitter pen collection (except for the mauve, pink and purple ones. She is NEVER getting those. Ever.)
Max	Barnaby B. Bear, my favorite one-eyed teddy
Nanna Kate	The "My Secret" perfume she gave me for my birthday two years ago (there is still quite a lot left in the bottle)

Name	What I am bequeathing them
BOB	My red shoes that he is always trying to chew up
Peach	(ex) BFF Nothing
ZOE	(ex) BFF An even bigger nothing

✳ Bequeathing means giving stuff to people that you won't need because you'll be too dead to use it.

I'm too distressed to write any more now, Diary. Maybe after dinner, if I am feeling strong enough.

Ella x

Sunday night, in bed

Dear Diary,

I am eating some chocolate cookies I found in the pantry. Who cares if I have nightmares (even ones with hairy, googly-eyed monsters in them)? My life is already a **big nightmare** RIGHT NOW.

Here's what happened.

I was taking Bob for a nice relaxing walk in the park today when I saw something Extremely Suspicious over near the ornamental fountain.

I immediately went into ninja
stealth mode and hid behind a
giant tree so I could Observe
the Suspicious Behavior
without being seen.*

* which is **extremely** hard to
do when you are holding a **very
bouncy, very licky** dog so he won't
bark and reveal your location or run over
to the person who is Behaving Suspiciously.

And guess who I Observed???

Zoe. Chatting and laughing and trying on
silly hats with her New Friend.

Zoe doesn't even **like** wearing hats.

And guess who her
New Friend is???

HINT: Her name is a type of ~~foot~~ jewel.

ha
HA
Ha

zoe

Monday, after school

Dear Diary,

I wish to announce that Zoe
is now officially my ex-BFF.

That is all.

Zoe

↑↑↑

EX-BFF

Monday, about twelve minutes later

~~It's because~~

Monday, about twenty minutes after that

Monday, about two minutes after that

Sooo—here's what happened.

When I got to school this morning Zoe was waiting for me in our special spot near the cypress trees, just like everything was **absolutely, completely, utterly, totally OK** and she hadn't spent practically the WHOLE WEEKEND being a traitorous traitor instead of a true and loyal BFF.

ZOE

There was so much I wanted to talk about with her. Like how **excited** and **happy** I was when Ms. Crosby chose me to do the pas de deux. And how she was doing learning all her lines. And how worried I was that I might make a mistake in my dance. Or that Don Tay might drop me. ☹

Here's what we said instead:

Zoe (brightly): Hi, Ella!
How was your weekend?
Me: Did you just say
something?
Zoe (puzzled): Huh?

ZOE
(ex-BFF)

Me: Ohhhh. So you're talking to me then.

Zoe (even more puzzled): Sure. (Pausing to wave back to her special New Friend, who was waving at her from the other side of the playground.) Why wouldn't I be?

Me: Why don't you just go away and leave me alone? You've **obviously** got more exciting things to do OVER THERE.

Zoe (checking her watch to see how much time was left before the bell went): Well, if you're sure? Ammy was going to go over my lines with me. We've got a **really important** rehearsal at lunchtime today.

Me (inside my brain): Ammy???

MY BRaiN

Me (out loud): One trillion percent sure. And you know what? You don't HAVE to be my BFF anymore.

Zoe: What? What are you talking about?

Me: You know EXACTLY what I'm talking about, Zo-ee.

Zoe: I do?

Me: Just forget we were ever friends, OK? You can be Ammy's BFF instead.

Zoe (rolling her eyes): You know what? I will.

Me: FINE!

Zoe: FINE!

And then we both stormed off like storming thunderstorms and we didn't say ONE WORD to each other for the WHOLE REST OF THE DAY.

Tuesday, after school

Still not speaking to Zoe.

Wednesday, after dinner

Still not speaking.

NOPE.

NOPE.

NOPE.

Thursday, after school

The phone rang and I raced to get it in case it was Zoe calling me to say sorry, but it was only Matilda calling to see if Olivia wanted to come over to play dolls. **Bleuchhhh.** Matilda and Olivia are such BABIES.

And anyway even if Zoe **DID** call to say sorry, I wouldn't say sorry back.

Not in a MILLION TRILLION YEARS.

Wednesday night, in bed, exhausted

Dearest Diary,

I'm so sorry I haven't written in you for a whole week, but I have been busy, busy, busy—like a busy bumblebee buzzing around, getting ready for our play.

BUSY
Bumblebee
(ME)

Guess what happened today!

Princess Peach was being a BIG SHOW-OFF while we were practicing our rope-climbing dance. She climbed up to the top of the climbing frame in the gym and fell off and hurt her ankle. And now she can't be in the play.

Peach at **TOP** OF Rigging

...and at the **BOTTOM**!

OWW!

I couldn't WAIT to tell Zoe all about it!

And then I remembered she's not my BFF anymore. So I didn't. ☹

Thursday night, in bed

Dear Diary,

Today, after school, Don Tay and I went to see Madame Fry (my old ballet teacher) and she gave us a private personal pas de deux lesson!

And Don Tay picked
me up and twirled me
over his head and he
only **ALMOST** dropped
me once.

So now I'm feeling a
WHOLE lot better about
our dance next week.

Good night, Diary.
Sweet dreams.
Ella xx

☺ ☺ ☺

ME!!

DON TAY

Friday night, after dinner

I was at the shopping center
with Mom and Olivia after
school today buying some new
shoes when we bumped into
Poppy and Georgia.

Poppy said she'd just seen
Amethyst with a lady and two
little girls that looked just like
Amethyst (except they weren't
wearing anything purple) in the
Do Drop In Coffee Shoppe—and
they were sitting with Mr. Martini!

Zow-ee! I wonder if she's in trouble again???

As soon as I got home I raced into
the kitchen and called
Zoe to find out MORE
INFORMATION.

And then I remembered Zoe
and I aren't **ever** speaking to each other
again. Ever. We don't even talk to each other
in class, which is EXTREMELY hard to do
when you are sitting at the same table for
practically THE WHOLE DAY.

So I hung up before she had a chance to
pick up. ☹

Sunday night, in bed, very late

Dear Diary,

I am desperately trying to go to sleep and I can't.

I miss Zoe—REALLY, REALLY badly.

Mom said I was being silly and I should have called her this morning and asked her to come over. But Zoe was probably busy, I thought.

Busy doing something with Ammy.

E

Monday night, late

Dear Diary,

I can't sleep again tonight but this time it's because **I AM SO EXCITED!**

So excited

We had our dress rehearsal for the play! Which means I **FINALLY** got to wear my stylish, floaty pas de deux dress. And it is a**MAZing**! And **BEAUTiful!** And ~~GORJus~~ **GORGeous!** It makes me feel just like a (pirate) princess.

Stylish
floaty ♥

♥Pirate
PRINCESS

♥Pas de Deux
DRESS

Even Amethyst told me it was amazing.
And she wished me good luck for tomorrow
night. (Zoe didn't. ☹)

We did a run-through✱ of the play.

✱ A run-through means you practice the
whole play with all the singing and dancing
and acting and costumes. It does NOT
mean you run across the stage screaming
like zombies with their heads cut off.

Amethyst was REALLY good. You could tell why the teachers chose her to be Captain Swashbuckler.

Zoe was good too. Except I could tell she was REALLY nervous, because her right knee was shaking like the coconuts in a coconut tree when a big wind is blowing at them. Zoe's knee ALWAYS does that when she's nervous.

I can't wait for tomorrow night!

Wednesday night, very late

Dearest Diary,

We did the play!

The actors acted and said "Aaaaarrrrrr!" and "Ahoy, me hearties" a lot.

And the dancers who were the ship's rats ran around the stage and made everyone laugh (especially when they accidentally on purpose bumped into each other).

After all my **special dances** with the Group A girls (except for Princess Peach, of course, who sat scowling in the audience with her foot up on a cushion), I did my pas de deux with Don Tay. And he didn't drop me. Not even once!

And Nanna Kate gave Mr. Zugaro some flowers to give to me on the stage. As if I was a REAL STAR! And I got to take a bow on stage with all the people with main parts.

Real ★
STAR ★

And guess what?

You never will so I'll just tell you.

Just before the curtain went up, Zoe got stage fright and she was **too scared** to go on! Her right knee started shaking again, and her voice went all trembly, and her face went white, just like a gigantic marshmallow.

Marshmallow
FACE

Trembly
Voice

Shaky
Knee

So I went over and patted her gently on the arm and whispered, "Don't be scared, Zoe. You can do ANYTHING," just like we were still BFFs.

You can do ANYTHING.

And then I ran off to get ready for my first dance.

And guess what else?

Zoe stopped being nervous and was really, really good. Ms. Weiss said she was the best Mabel she'd ever seen. Ever.

PS (five minutes later)

Oops. I forgot to tell you.

Mr. Martini is actually Amethyst Merryweather's DAD!

Poppy heard Mr. Martini talking to Ms. Weiss about Amethyst. And guess what? She had to leave her other school and come to ours! And then Poppy told Georgia and Georgia told Chloe and Chloe told me.

MR. MARTINI

Principal=
DAD

And her real WHOLE name is actually Amethyst Martini Merryweather!! OBVIOUSLY Amethyst doesn't want anyone to know that HER DAD is the SCHOOL PRINCIPAL. That would be just WEIRD.

★AMETHYST★
MARTiNi
MERRYWEATHER

But that explains EVERYTHING about why Ammy is SO mysTERious (and sits outside Mr. M.'s office a lot, even though she NEVER gets in trouble).

I wonder if she needs another friend?

PPS (five minutes after that)

And guess what else?

Zoe and I both said a **very sorrowful sorry** to each other. At exactly the same time.

And now we're talking to each other again.

Diaries

Read more of Ella's brilliant diary